Fossils

Connor Dayton

PowerKiDS
press™

New York

Published in 2007 by The Rosen Publishing Group, Inc.
29 East 21st Street, New York, NY 10010

First Edition

Editor: Jennifer Way
Book Design: Greg Tucker

Photo Credits: Cover, pp. 5, 7, 9, 11, 11 (inset), 15, 19, 21 Shutterstock.com; p. 13 © Tim Boyle/Getty Images; p. 17 © Laski Diffusion/EastNews/Liaison/Getty Images.

Library of Congress Cataloging-in-Publication Data

Dayton, Connor.
  Fossils / Connor Dayton. — 1st ed.
      p. cm. — (Rocks and minerals)
  Includes index.
  ISBN-13: 978-1-4042-3689-9 (library binding)
  ISBN-10: 1-4042-3689-9 (library binding)
  1. Fossils—Juvenile literature. 2. Paleontology—Juvenile literature. I. Title.
  QE714.5.D39 2007
  560—dc22
                                        2006030805

Manufactured in the United States of America

Contents

What Are Fossils?

Fossils are the **preserved** remains of living things that died **millions** of years ago. They can be the remains of plants, animals, or other **organisms**. Dinosaur bones are one kind of fossil you might know about. Fossils also can be the traces, or things left behind, of once-living organisms. These trace fossils can be things such as footprints or eggs.

Fossils can be found all over the world in different kinds of **sedimentary rocks**. The people who study fossils are called **paleontologists**.

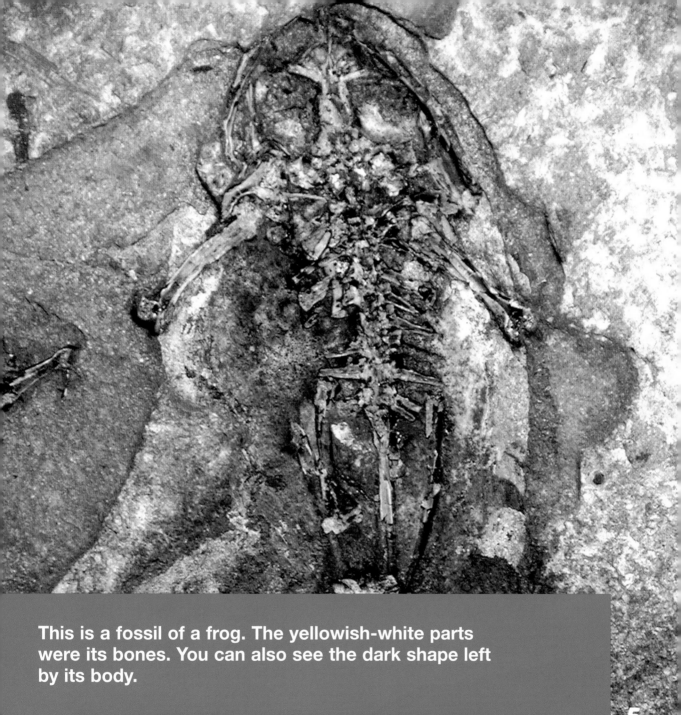

This is a fossil of a frog. The yellowish-white parts were its bones. You can also see the dark shape left by its body.

How Do Fossils Form?

Fossils form when **layers** of sediment build up on a dead organism. When a dead organism becomes part of these sedimentary layers, its shape gets pressed into the rock. This pressed shape will become a fossil.

Most dead organisms will not become fossils. They decay, or break down, before sediment can preserve their shape. There are more fossils of organisms that lived in lakes and oceans because sediment builds up faster under water than on land. There also are more fossils of organisms that were hard on the outside because they kept their shape better under the pressing of sediment.

There are many fossils of sea animals, such as fish, because sediment builds up quickly on the ocean floor. This allows the organism to be preserved and form a fossil.

Perimineralization

After an organism begins to be covered by sediment, the next step of fossilization begins. This step is called **perimineralization**. After an organism decays, water drips into the space that has been left behind. This water carries minerals with it and leaves them behind when it **evaporates**. Over time the minerals build up and harden. This fossilized rock takes the shape of the organism.

If an organism has not decayed very much before perimineralization begins, its fossil might look a lot like the living organism. If an animal's body has decayed a lot, only its bones and teeth will fossilize.

This is a close-up of a dinosaur's fossilized teeth. The fossil is so well preserved that it is exactly the same shape and size as the dinosaur's teeth were when it was living.

Compression Fossils and Replacement Fossils

Fossilization can happen in different ways to organisms. How it happens is decided by both the organism's form and the **conditions** under which fossilization happens.

Compression fossils can happen when sedimentary rocks form on top of plants. As the rock forms, it presses down hard on the organism. This preserves the shape of the organism.

Replacement fossils happen when the whole organism has decayed. This leaves a space in the rock that has the organism's shape. This is called a mold fossil. Sometimes the space in a rock gets filled with other minerals and hardens. This is called a cast fossil.

This leaf is a compression fossil. *Inset:* This replacement cast fossil is of an animal called a trilobite.

Paleontology

Paleontologists study the history of Earth. This makes learning about fossils important to them. Studying fossils tells paleontologists about the plants and animals that lived millions of years ago. They get fossils by digging into the ground and carefully removing the rock that is around them.

Paleontologists use **carbon dating** to figure out how long ago the fossilized organisms lived. By dating fossils, they can make a timeline of changes that have taken place on Earth. These are changes such as how Earth's weather has changed over time and when different plants and animals became extinct, or died out.

This life-size model shows a paleontologist carefully digging for dinosaur bones. Using small brushes and other tools, it can take months to remove a large animal's fossil.

Body Fossils

When a fossil is made of a whole organism, it is called a body fossil. Body fossils can be shells from sea animals or whole plants. They can even be dinosaurs!

Body fossils interest paleontologists because they can see what the organism looked like when it was alive. They can study body fossils to **compare** them to other fossils from the same time period. Doing this helps paleontologists put together an idea of what life was like millions of years ago. They can also compare body fossils to see if they are like any organisms that are living today!

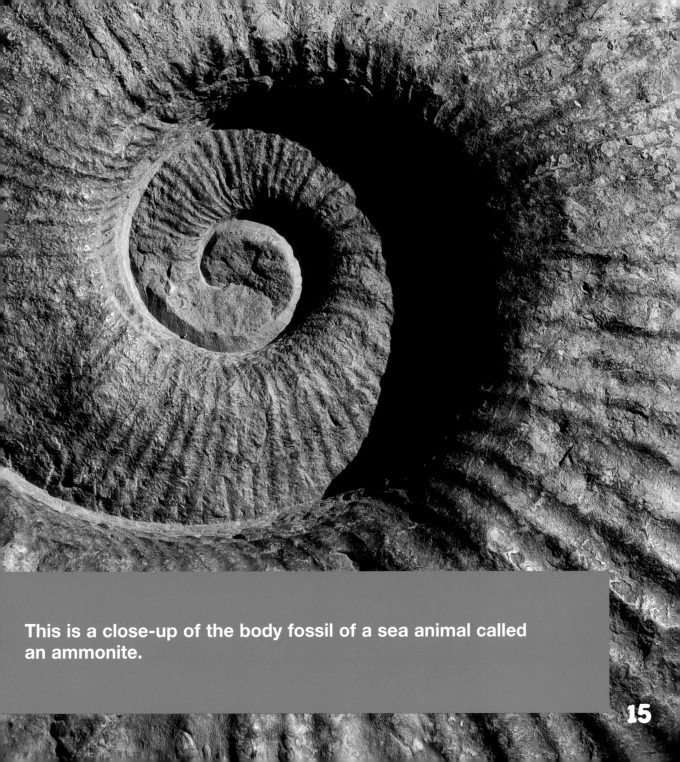

This is a close-up of the body fossil of a sea animal called an ammonite.

Trace Fossils

Sometimes an animal leaves behind things that become fossilized. These kinds of fossils are known as trace fossils. Trace fossils can be footprints or eggs. Even animal droppings can become trace fossils!

Trace fossils give paleontologists many clues about animals that lived millions of years ago. A fossilized footprint can show how big an animal was and how much it weighed. A fossilized egg can show what an animal's young looked like. Fossilized droppings can give clues about what an animal ate.

Here is a fossilized dinosaur egg. You can see broken pieces of the egg's shell. The inside of the egg has turned into rock.

Dinosaurs

One of the most interesting types of fossils are dinosaurs. There were many different kinds of dinosaurs. Some kinds ate meat. Other kinds ate plants. Some dinosaurs walked on four legs. Other kinds walked on two legs. There were dinosaurs that lived in the water and dinosaurs that lived on land. Some kinds of dinosaurs even had wings and flew!

Dinosaurs became extinct around 65 million years ago. Some dinosaurs are believed to have things in common with today's birds and **reptiles**. Paleontologists learned all these things about dinosaurs through studying their fossils.

This is a fossilized dinosaur skeleton in a museum. A skeleton is the set of bones that make up the shape of an animal's body.

Other Kinds of Fossils

Microfossils, fossilized resin, and petrified wood are examples of other types of fossils. Microfossils are fossils that are too small to be studied without special tools. Microfossils can be whole organisms, such as tiny animals that lived in the ocean. They can also be tiny parts from larger organisms, such as spores from plants.

Fossilized resin, or amber, comes from tree sap. Sometimes bugs or other small animals get trapped and preserved in amber.

Petrified wood is a fossilized tree. Minerals have hardened in the tree's shape. The Petrified Forest in Arizona has lots of these fossils.

Here is a piece of petrified wood. You can see that the fossil has taken the shape of the tree, down to the tree's rings. This kind of fossil can tell paleontologists what Earth was like when the tree was alive.

Index

Web Sites

Due to the changing nature of Internet links, PowerKids Press has developed an online list of Web sites related to the subject of this book. This site is updated regularly. Please use this link to access the list:
www.powerkidslinks.com/romi/foss/